Friends of the
Houston Public Library

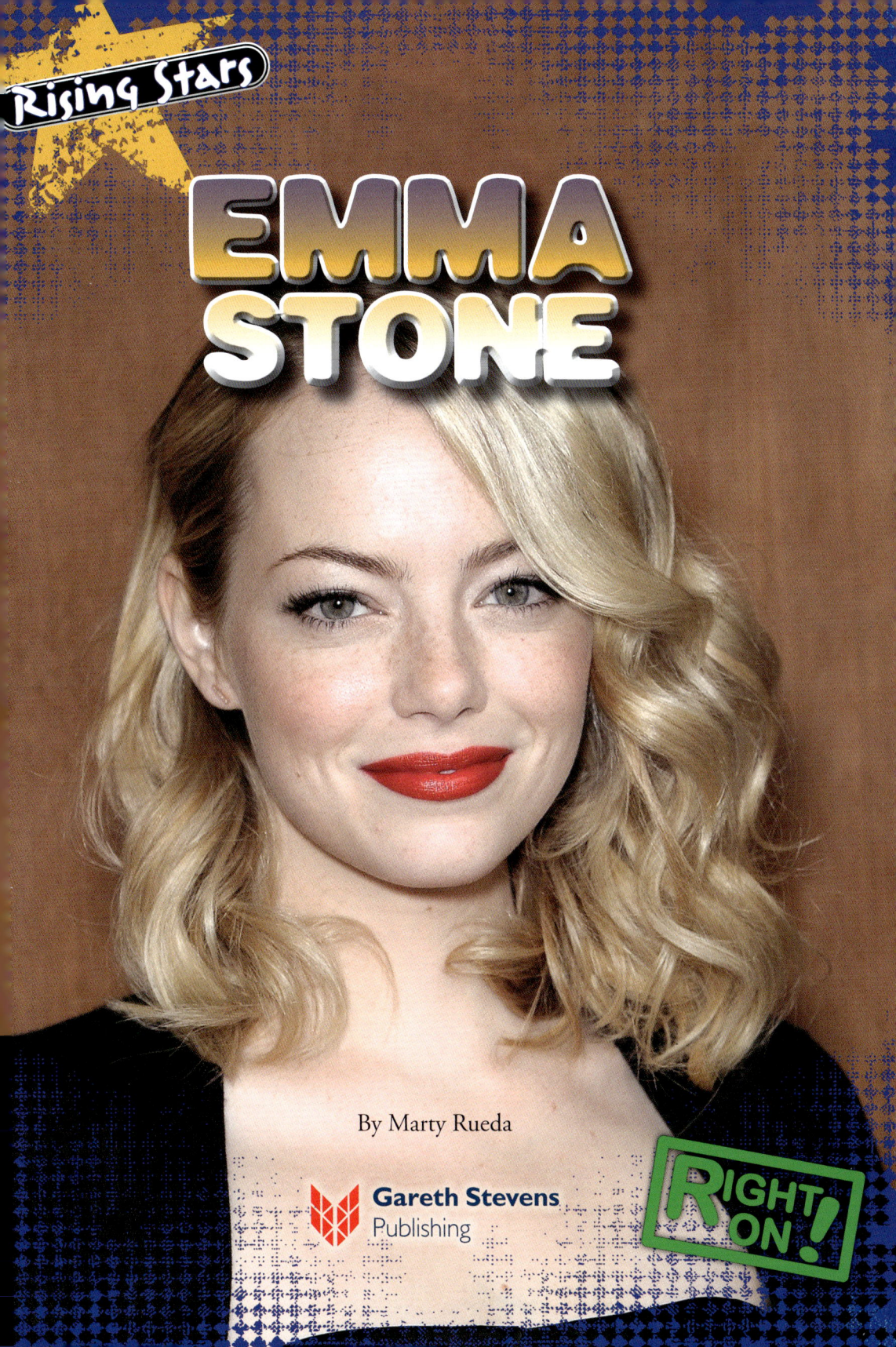

Please visit our website, www.garethstevens.com. For a free color catalog of all our high-quality books, call toll free 1-800-542-2595 or fax 1-877-542-2596.

Rueda, Marty.
Emma Stone / by Marty Rueda.
    p. cm. — (Rising stars)
Includes index.
 ISBN 978-1-4339-8974-2 (pbk.)
ISBN 978-1-4339-8975-9 (6-pack)
ISBN 978-1-4339-8973-5 (library binding)
1. Stone, Emma,—1988—Juvenile literature. 2. Actors—United States—Biography—Juvenile literature. I. Title.
PN2287.S73 R84 2014
921—d23

First Edition

Published in 2014 by Gareth Stevens Publishing
111 East 14th Street, Suite 349
New York, NY 10003

Copyright © 2014 Gareth Stevens Publishing

Designer: Nick Domiano
Editor: Therese Shea

Photo credits: Cover, p. 1 Dominique Charriau/WireImage/Getty Images; p. 5 Andy Kropa/Getty Images Entertainment/Getty Images; p. 7 Alberto E. Rodriguez/Getty Images Entertainment/Getty Images; p. 9 Sean Gallup/Getty Images Entertainment/Getty Images; p. 11 Bryan Bedder/Getty Images Entertainment/Getty Images; p. 13 Jason Merritt/Getty Images Entertainment/Getty Images; p. 15 Carlos Alvarez/Getty Images Entertainment/Getty Images; p. 17 Cindy Ord/Getty Images Entertainment/Getty Images; p. 19 Juan Naharro Gimenez/WireImage/Getty Images; p. 21 Kevin Winter/Getty Images Entertainment/Getty Images; p. 23 GERARD JULIEN/AFP/Getty Images; p. 25 Lester Cohen/WireImage/Getty Images; p. 27 Bobby Bank/WireImage/Getty Images; p. 29 Kevin Mazur/WireImage/Getty Images.

All rights reserved. No part of this book may be reproduced in any form without permission in writing from the publisher, except by a reviewer.

Printed in the United States of America

CPSIA compliance information: Batch #CS13GS: For further information contact Gareth Stevens, New York, New York at 1-800-542-2595.

A Funny Star	4
Emily Jean	6
A Big Move	12
From TV to Movies	16
Leading Lady	18
Major Star	26
Timeline	30
For More Information	31
Glossary	32
Index	32

A Funny Star

Emma Stone loves to make people laugh. She wanted to be an actor so she could do just that.

Emily Jean

Emma's real name is Emily Jean Stone. She was born in Scottsdale, Arizona, on November 6, 1988.

Emma wanted to be an actor when she was just 4 years old! She and her dad loved to watch comedies together.

When Emma was 11, she began acting on stage. She was in more than 15 shows! She did a comedy act, too.

A Big Move

When Emma was 15, she told her parents she wanted to go to Hollywood. She wanted to become an actor. They said yes!

In 2003, Emma and her mother moved to Los Angeles, California. She auditioned for many TV shows. She didn't get any parts.

From TV to Movies

In 2004, Emma was on a talent show. She sang and won a part in the TV show *The New Partridge Family*. This helped her get other roles.

Leading Lady

In 2009, Emma had a big part in the movie *Zombieland*. Soon, Emma got other movie roles.

In 2010, Emma was on the TV show *Saturday Night Live*. She said that was a dream come true.

By 2010, many people knew Emma could play lead roles in movies. She even won an MTV Movie Award in 2011!

In 2011, Emma got her first serious role in *The Help*. She played a young writer in the 1960s.

Major Star

In 2012, Emma played her biggest role yet. She was Gwen Stacy in *The Amazing Spider-Man*.

Emma knows many famous people. Taylor Swift is one of her good friends! What's next for this funny girl?

Timeline

1988 Emily Jean Stone is born on November 6 in Arizona.

2003 Emma and her mom move to Los Angeles.

2004 Emma wins a talent show.

2009 Emma appears in *Zombieland*.

2010 Emma hosts *Saturday Night Live*.

2011 Emma wins her first MTV Movie Award.

2011 Emma has a serious role in *The Help*.

2012 Emma stars in *The Amazing Spider-Man*.

Books

Schuman, Michael A. *Emma! Amazing Actress Emma Stone*. Berkeley Heights, NJ: Enslow Publishers, 2013.

Tieck, Sarah. *Emma Stone: Talented Actress*. Minneapolis, MN: ABDO Publishing, 2013.

Websites

Emma Stone

www.people.com/people/emma_stone/

Read the latest news about Emma.

Emma Stone

www.imdb.com/name/nm1297015/

Learn what new movies Emma will be starring in.

Publisher's note to educators and parents: Our editors have carefully reviewed these websites to ensure that they are suitable for students. Many websites change frequently, however, and we cannot guarantee that a site's future contents will continue to meet our high standards of quality and educational value. Be advised that students should be closely supervised whenever they access the Internet.

audition: to try out

comedy: a movie, play, or book meant to make people laugh

serious: dealing with matters in a thoughtful way, not trying to be funny

talent: skills or gifts

actor 4, 8, 12
Amazing Spider-Man, The 26, 30
Arizona 6, 30
comedies 8
comedy act 10
Help, The 24, 30
Hollywood 12
Los Angeles, California 14, 30
movies 18, 22
MTV Movie Award 22, 30
New Partridge Family, The 16
Saturday Night Live 20, 30
stage 10
Stone, Emily Jean 6, 30
talent show 16, 30
TV 14, 16, 20
Zombieland 18, 30

B S877R   Friends of the   CEN
Rueda, Marty, Houston Public Library
Emma Stone /

CENTRAL LIBRARY
11/14